THE ROAD TO BETHLEHEM

BRIAN WILDSMITH

OXFORD
UNIVERSITY PRESS

It was spring, and God sent the angel Gabriel to Nazareth to visit a young girl called Mary.

'You will have a son,' he said. 'His name will be Jesus and he will be called the Son of God.'

Some time later, Mary and her husband Joseph had to go to Bethlehem.
As it was a long way, Mary could not take her cat and dog with her, so she
left them with a neighbour to look after.

The cat and the dog missed Mary very much. So one day they ran away to try and find her.

On their way they met a fox. He was stuck fast in a rabbit hole. Cat and Dog wanted to help him, so they pulled and pulled until Fox was free.

'Oh, thank you,' said Fox. 'Where are you going to?'

'To Bethlehem to find Mary.'

'Can I come too?'

'Yes, just follow us,' they replied. And off they went.

On their way they met a goat. He had got stuck in a cart while trying to steal some carrots. Cat, Dog, and Fox all wanted to help him, so they pulled and pulled until Goat was free.

'Oh, thank you,' said Goat. 'Where are you going to?'
'To Bethlehem to find Mary.'
'Can I come too?'
'Yes, just follow us,' they replied. And off they went.

On their way they met a bear. He had been
caught in a hunter's trap while trying to steal honey
from a bees' nest. Cat, Dog, and Fox all wanted to help
him, so they pulled and pulled until Bear was free.
   'Oh, thank you,' said Bear. 'Where are you going to?'
   'To Bethlehem to find Mary.'
   'Can I come too?'
   'Yes, just follow us,' they replied. And off they went.

They came to a big palace and there they met three camels.

'Where are you going to?' said the camels.

'To Bethlehem to find Mary.'

'We'd like to come with you,' said the camels. 'But we have to wait here for our masters.'

'Perhaps we'll meet again,' said Cat, Dog, Fox, Goat, and Bear. 'Goodbye.'

As they came near to Bethlehem, they met some sheep, grazing in a field.

'Where are you going to?' said the sheep.

'To Bethlehem to find Mary.'

'So are we. We know the way. Just follow us.'

When they reached Bethlehem, they could not see Mary in the inn.
Instead they found her in the stable with her new-born baby.

Mary was delighted to see Cat and Dog and their friends.
'Come in,' she said, 'and meet my baby. His name is Jesus.'

Then the three camels arrived, carrying three kings.
'We have followed a shining star,' said the kings. And kneeling down,
they offered the baby their gifts of gold, frankincense, and myrrh.

'Our journey is ended now,' said Cat and Dog. 'We have found Mary and
her baby Jesus, who is the Son of God.'

OXFORD

UNIVERSITY PRESS

Great Clarendon Street, Oxford CX2 6DP

Oxford University Press is a department of the University of Oxford.
It furthers the University's objective of excellence in research, scholarship,
and education by publishing worldwide in

Oxford New York

Auckland Bangkok Buenos Aires Cape Town Chennai
Dar es Salaam Delhi Hong Kong Istanbul Karachi Kolkata
Kuala Lumpur Madrid Melbourne Mexico City Mumbai Nairobi
São Paulo Shanghai Taipei Tokyo Toronto

Oxford is a registered trade mark of Oxford University Press
in the UK and in certain other countries

British Library Cataloguing in Publication Data available

ISBN 0-19-279098-6 Hardback
ISBN 0-19-272553-X Paperback

1 3 5 7 9 10 8 6 4 2

Printed in Dai Nippon, Hong Kong

PIANO PIECES FOR CHILDREN

Yorktown Music Press
London/New York/Sydney

Exclusive Distributors:
Music Sales Limited
8/9 Frith Street, London W1V 5TZ, England
Music Sales Pty. Limited
120 Rothschild Avenue, Rosebery, N.S.W. 2018, Australia

This book © copyright 1981 by
Yorktown Music Press
ISBN. 0.86001.989.6
Order No. YK 20212

Designed by Howard Brown
Cover illustration by Keith Richens

Music Sales complete catalogue lists thousands of titles
and is free from your local music bookshop, or direct from
Music Sales Limited. Please send a cheque or Postal Order for
£1.50 for postage to Music Sales Limited, 8/9 Frith Street,
London W1V 5TZ.

Printed in England by:
Dotesios Ltd., Trowbridge, Wiltshire

Piano Pieces for Children

CONTENTS

French Child's Song

Franz Behr

"Surprise" Symphony Theme from the Andante

Joseph Haydn

Grade I

Melody Op. 68

Robert Schumann

Grade I

The Harebell

William Smallwood

Grade I

Home Sweet Home

Henry Rowley Bishop

Grade II

Andante

Last Rose Of Summer

Grade II

Friedrich von Flotow

Larghetto

Gavotte In D

Johann Sebastian Bach

Cradle Song

Carl Maria von Weber

Grade II

Andante

Auld Lang Syne

Grade II

Moderato

Cradle Song

Grade II

Johannes Brahms

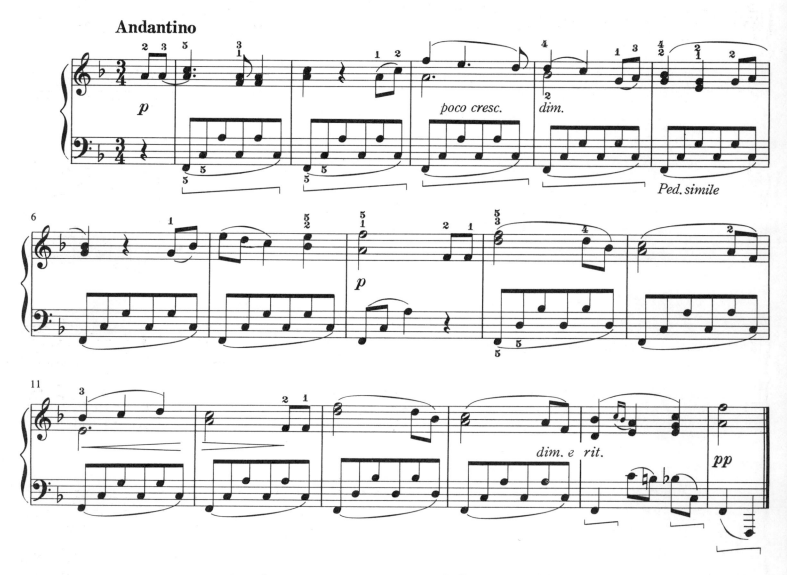

Theme From "Oberon"

Grade II

Carl Maria von Weber

poco rit. e dim.

13

Musette

Johann Sebastian Bach

Grade II

Melody In F

Anton Rubinstein

Sonatina Op. 36, No. 1

Muzio Clementi

Grade II

Love's Old Sweet Song

James Lyman Molloy

Grade II

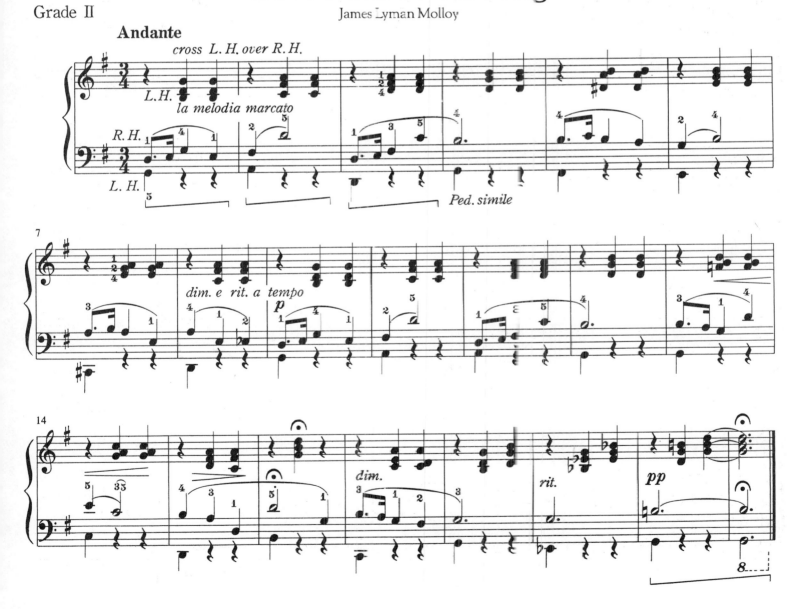

Little Fairy Waltz Op. 105, No. 1

Grade II

Ludovic Streabbog

Peasant Dance Op. 208, No. 5

Grade II

Friedrich Baumfelde

Soldiers' March

Robert Schumann

Tulip Op. 111, No. 4

Grade II

Heinrich Lichner

25

At Home Op. 134, No. 6

Grade II

Heinrich Lichner

Allegro moderato

D.S. al Fine
poi la Trio

D.S. 𝄋 al Fine
poi la Coda

Gertrude's Dream Waltz

Grade II

Ludwig van Beethoven

(∗) Small hands may omit the octave span, and play the lower note of the octave only.

Londonderry Air

Grade II

Spring Song

Felix Mendelssohn

Grade III

Allegretto grazioso

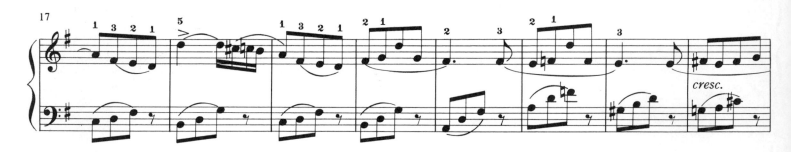

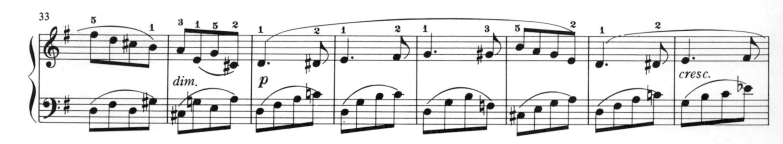

Consolation Op. 30, No. 3

Felix Mendelssohn

Grade III

Doll's Dream

Theodore Oesten

Grade III
Cradle Song.
Andante con moto

The doll sleeps.

aim. e rall.

The doll's dream.
Moderato

35

The doll wakes.

The doll dances.
Allegretto moderato

Für Elise

Ludwig van Beethoven

Grade III

Largo

George Frederic Händel

Grade III

Album Leaf

Edvard Grieg

Grade III

The Fountain Op. 221

Karl Bohm

Grade III

Allegretto

Knight Rupert

Robert Schumann

Grade III

Minuet In G

Ludwig van Beethoven

Grade III

D.S. %: al Fine

La Paloma

Sebastien Yracier

Grade III

Grandmother's Minuet Op. 68, No. 2

Edvard Grieg

Grade III

Allegretto grazioso e leggierissimo

Träumerei

Robert Schumann

Valse Lente from the ballet "Coppélia"

Grade III

Leo Delibes

Gipsy Dance

Heinrich Lichner

Allegro agitato

Waltz In A♭ Op. 39, No. 15

Johannes Brahms

Grade III

Venetian Boat Song No. 2 Op. 30, No. 6

Felix Mendelssohn

Grade III

Allegretto tranquillo

Camp Of The Gypsies Op. 424, No. 3

Franz Behr

Grade III

Allegretto con moto

Tarantella

A. Pieczonka

Grade IV

Ecossaises

Ludwig van Beethoven/Busoni

Grade IV

The Beautiful Blue Danube

Grade IV

Johann Strauss Jr.

Tempo di Valse

Chaconne

Auguste Durand

Allegretto

Sonatina

Daniel Gottlob Türk

Grade IV

1/93 (14953)

The Beatles
 Enya

 Phil Collins
 Van Morrison
 Bob Dylan

 Sting
 Paul Simon
 Tracy Chapman

 Eric Clapton
 Pink Floyd
 New Kids On The Block

 Bryan Adams
 Tina Turner
 Elton John

 Bee Gees
 Whitney Houston
 AC/DC

Bringing you the words

All the latest in rock and pop. Plus the brightest and best in West End show scores. Music books for every instrument under the sun. And exciting new teach-yourself ideas like "Let's Play Keyboard" - in cassette/book packs, or on video. Available from all good music shops.

and music

Music Sales' complete catalogue lists thousands of titles and is available free from your local music shop, or direct from Music Sales Limited. Please send a cheque or postal order for £1.50 (for postage) to:

Music Sales Limited
Newmarket Road,
Bury St Edmunds,
Suffolk IP33 3YB

 **Buddy**
 **Five Guys Named Moe**
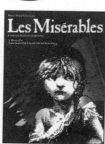 **Les Misérables**
 **West Side Story**

 **Phantom Of The Opera**
 **Show Boat**
 The Rocky Horror Show

Bringing you the world's best music.